A FLYING KISS

"Hello, We welcome the passengers onboard and request you to listen and follow the instructions from one of our staffs for your smooth journey."

These were the first words that was announced on the British Airways flight BA 138 which was scheduled to depart from Mumbai to New York within few minutes.

All the passengers fastened their seat belts and the plane slowly moved towards the runway.

It was night time and the passengers could see the airport fully lighted and also the flashing lights beneath the planes flashing as some of them landed and skidded through the runway.

It waited for a few minutes as the flight scheduled before this one was yet to take off which it did eventually.

All of a sudden, the British Airways BA 138 just pulled the gear and the flight began to run through the run way heading for the take off.

It ran for nearly four kilometers and slowly lifted up in the air. The passengers could feel the movement and some children who had window seats could see the aerial view of the lights of the runway which turned smaller in size as the flight elevated into the sky.

"Hello, This is Captain Avinash with my colleague Mr. James Matthews." announced Avinash who was working with British Airways for the last few years and he was known for handling emergencies during the flights in a well manner.

Avinash was in nature simple and was social with people as he believed that his profession requires him to be social with others irrespective of him being social or not.

Soon as the flight was 40,000 feet above, Avinash set the plane on autopilot mode and bid good night to the passengers and himself went to sleep though he knew he is not supposed to go to sleep for long hours during duty.

After flying for nearly four hours, an announcement was made by one of the air hostess informing the passengers that they are soon going to land at New York City.

The city was as busy as usual. The plane landed on the runway no. 4 and headed nearly three kilometers before it slowed down and took a right and stopped.

The airstairs were brought and the doors were opened and all the passengers disembarked.

Once the flight was vacant, Avinash came out from the cockpit and went to the washroom to get freshen up.

"How was your flight sir?" asked one of the air hostess who usually accompanied him on most of the duties.

"It was fine. How about yours?" asked Avinash.

"Do I need to reply? Don't you know that whenever I am on duty with you, I need not fear for my life even at 40,000 feet height." replied smiling.

Avinash nodded and went to the stairs and disembarked and went to the airport.

A car was waiting for him to take him to the hotel. Avinash took his baggage and sat at the rear of the car and headed towards to the hotel.

"Welcome sir, Your room number is 426." said the receptionist handing him the keys. He took his baggage and went upstairs to his room.

He opened the door and kept his baggage just near the door and went in and got freshened up once again.

After getting freshened up he just lay on the bed and went off to sleep.

His door bell rang and Avinash woke up and opened the door.

"Sir, your dinner has arrived." said waiter who was standing in the lobby with dinner in a trolley which was covered with cloth.

"You may keep it here." said Avinash and once the waiter left, Avinash opened the cover of the dinner.

The dinner was Indian as Avinash always preferred Indian dish though abroad and he loved to eat Naan and Palak paneer very much.

After a break of a day, he was supposed to report back on duty and return to Mumbai by the same flight.

As usual he went into the cockpit and checked the required parameters which were part of preflight checks.

"Hey do you know that a new air hostess has joined the crew today. Any idea?" said James Mathews.

"Really? I had no idea about it at all." replied Avinash

"She is in the galley. Go and have a look." said James smiling and making a joke.

"No need for that. She will come here on her own." said Avinash.

"You gonna call her here?" asked James again.

"Not at all. Just wait and watch. If we are lucky she will come here on her own. Just check our luck." said Avinash winking his eye.

The flight departed on schedule and was above in mid air.

"Sir, would like to have something?" came a voice from behind.

Avinash turned back and saw a girl who seemed Indian and was standing near the cockpit door which was partially closed to avoid passengers peeping inside the cockpit.

The girl seemed disciplined and was really beautiful. Her beauty was really to be admired. She had applied lipsticks on her lips and also eyelashes which added to her beauty. Not a single pimple was visible on her face.

She was wearing her dark blue uniforms which consisted of blue mini skirt and a white shirt with a blue overcoat.

"Sir, would you like to have something?" she asked again.

"Hmm a cup of coffee." replied Avinash after some thinking.

"Anything else sir?" she asked again.

"No, nothing. This is ok." said Avinash smiling.

She closed the door and went back to the galley to fetch the coffee.

Avinash was smiling himself thinking of her while the door of cockpit opened again.

"Here's your coffee sir", she said and turned around to leave.

"Just a minute", said Avinash.

She turned back.

"May I know your name?" asked Avinash politely.

"Avantika Sharma." she replied and smiled broadly.

"Are you a new joinee?" asked Avinash.

"Yes sir. This is my third time on duty." replied Avantika.

"I am Avinash." said Avinash and shook hands with her while introducing himself.

After some time Avinash called Avantika to cockpit and told her to make an announcement that they were to land soon.

After a span of twenty minutes the plane landed at Chhatrapati Shivaji International Airport.

"We hope you have enjoyed your flight with us." announced Avantika as the stairs proceeded towards the plane.

"Her voice is also beautiful as she." said Avinash to James who was hearing the announcement made by Avantika.

Just then Avantika came in with a piece of paper and handed it to Avinash.

"What is this?" asked Avinash.

"One of the passengers has given this to me and asked it to be forwarded to you. She says this is a thank you note for making her journey pleasant." said Avantika who was experiencing this kind of stuffs for the first time in her life.

"Did you read it?" asked Avinash.

"No sir, this is meant for you. So I didn't read it." replied Avantika.

Avinash opened the letter and began to read:

Respected Sir,

I don't know who you are but I am thankful to you for making my journey from New York to Mumbai pleasant.

Actually I have travelled in planes a lot of times but never had such an experience like this one. Also the air hostess who will be handing this letter to you was polite not only to me but to all passengers.

Thank you once again sir.

Merissa Stone.

Avinash gave back the letter to Avantika.

"The passenger has written about you." he said.

Thinking it would be like complain made to the captain regarding poor service by the air hostess, Avantika became sorrow.

"What happened?" asked Avinash as Avantika did not take the letter from him.

"Is it a complaint sir?" asked Avantika.

"Complaint? Regarding whom? This is a thank you note given by the passenger for good service done by you onboard." replied Avinash smiling loudly.

"Oh I thought it was a complaint that she might have written about me." said Avantika and also informed that she had not experienced like this before as she was new to this job.

Mumbai was the home town of both Avinash and Avantika. Avinash stayed at Colaba which is considered to be place of riches.

Avantika stayed at Mira Road in an apartment. Avantika's family consisted of her parents and her sister.

Her parents always supported in her career. Avantika always dreamt of becoming a pilot from childhood but could not afford the fees of pilot training so she opted for an air hostess job which too she believed would let her fly.

On the other hand, Avinash was rich from birth. He too dreamt of becoming a pilot and succeeded in achieving in dream without any hurdles.

"Mom, I am having duty tomorrow evening." said Avantika to her mother.

"I don't know why you love this job which just involves serving food to passengers." said her mother.

"Mom, there is a service beyond that which you will not understand." replied Avantika.

The next evening Avinash too was supposed to board the same flight as that of Avantika.

"Dad, you know a new air hostess has joined the crew that goes to USA frequently." said Avinash to his father.

"Really? How's she?" asked his father.

"Her name is Avantika Sharma. You know one thing? I have not seen any polite air hostess like her. Even her voice is so soft as a child." said Avinash describing her as is telling a story to his father.

"Don't forget that you have to board again tomorrow evening." said his father who has seen his son so happy for the first time.

"Yes dad, I know." replied Avinash and went to his room.

Avinash had simulation equipment in his room in which he practiced the route from Mumbai to New York most of the time when he was at home.

Avinash switched on the simulation equipment and was about to begin when his cell phone rang.

"Hello." said Avinash.

"Hi, James here. I have called you to tell some news." said James

"What's it?" asked Avinash.

"Can you come to our office at Andheri?' asked James.

"For what?" asked Avinash.

"I have got the details of Avantika Sharma." said James.

"Oh really? Or are you joking?" asked Avinash trying to figure if he was not joking.

"Oh man, I am serious. Can you come?" asked James once again.

"Yes, I am coming in an hour. You just be there." replied Avinash and disconnected the phone.

He took his car and went to Andheri. The road was congested with traffic and he reached Andheri after one and a half hour.

"Where is James?" he asked the receptionist at the office.

"He is waiting at the second floor." she responded.

Avinash went to the second floor where James was talking to another colleague and on seeing Avinash, James took him to a room and made him sit on a table.

"Tell me what details have you got?" asked Avinash enthusiastically.

He was so interested in Avantika that only James could feel the enthusiasm.

"Why are you so interested in knowing about her?" asked James just to irk Avinash.

"Who told I am interested in knowing about her?" said Avinash.

"Oh if that is so then why did you come to Andheri from Colaba?" said James again trying to irk Avinash more.

Trying not to lose his calm, Avinash responded back.

"There is nothing like what you are thinking." said Avinash.

"Well I thought, Avinash and Avantika would make a nice couple as the name too sounds similar. If there is nothing like that then I don't think giving you the details of her is proper." joked James.

"OK I accept, I am defeated. Now show me the details you have got." said Avinash who was getting more eager to know about her each time her name came to his ears.

James gave him a file which contained the list of air hostesses working with British Airways.

Avinash glanced through the names of air hostesses mentioned in the index.

AVANTIKA SHARMA, Page – 67: the index mentioned.

He immediately turned to Page No. 67 and saw the form filled out by her during her joining in the airlines.

He went through the details and came to know that she came from a middle class family.

Avinash thanked James for the details he got through him.

"What's you next move?" asked James.

"My next move is to go slow and steady. I cannot rush like the way you think." said Avinash.

"Anyway, I will always be there to support you whenever you need me." said James and both left the office.

The next evening Avinash reported for duty and was trying to check if Avantika is too on the same flight.

He was lucky that day as she too was on the same flight as Avinash and when she came into the flight she first greeted him with a Hi.

Avinash responded back and congratulated his stars for his luckiness.

Soon as usual the passengers boarded the plane and the plane took off the runway of the Mumbai airport.

Once the plane landed at the New York airport, Avinash wanted to go for a shopping as he sometimes does.

This time he shopped and brought a ring worth $87 which he thought he would gift to Avantika on her birthday which was soon to come after two weeks.

He called James and told him that he had planned to arrange a party at Hotel Taj which is located near the Gateway of India on Avantika's birthday.

"Do you think she will accept such a costly birthday bash?" asked James doubtedly.

"We will give her a surprise." replied Avinash.

"Well I will too come there. You just tell me when I should come?" asked James.

"Be there on 10th of July evening at 7 pm." said Avinash.

"Are you sure she don't have any schedule on that day." asked James in order to confirm.

"That I will check when I will be back to India tomorrow. Mostly she won't be having according to my estimation." said Avinash.

Avinash came back to the hotel and was getting bored as he had nothing to do except to sleep but he could not sleep either as whenever he tried to sleep the image of Avantika would flash in his mind.

The next day Avinash returned to Mumbai and went to his home.

He called the British Airways office and tried to confirm the duty schedule of Avantika and he came to know that on 10th of July, she did not have any duty and she was in USA on that day.

Avinash called again James to inform him that on her birthday Avantika is in USA on her birthday and not in India as he had expected.

"So what are you going to do now?" asked James.

"You suggest me some plans." said Avinash.

"Why don't you arrange a party in USA?" asked James again.

"Yes, that could be done. I never thought of it." replied Avinash thanking James for his idea.

"When are you starting preparations for that?" asked James eagerly.

"After two days I am going to USA again. I will ask the hotel where I stay about the party." said Avinash.

Two days went like two years for Avinash. He could not wait for making the arrangement for the birthday of Avantika which he was to throw as a surprise for her.

On duty he flew to New York and discussed with the manager of the hotel regarding the surprise birthday party.

For two weeks Avinash felt restless. He was regularly keeping in touch with the manager of the hotel regarding the preparation for the party.

Finally the day arrived. Avinash and Avantika were on the same flight on duty when they landed at New York, the day before her birthday.

"Avantika, what are your plans tomorrow?" asked Avinash.

"Well sir, nothing special. As usual I will be in the hotel. Why?" she asked.

"If you don't mind, you can come to have dinner with James and me." said Avinash.

"Really?" asked Avantika suddenly her face shone when she said this.

"I am not joking at all." said Avinash smiling.

"I will definitely come." said Avantika and bid goodbye to both Avinash and James.

"Finally you are on the runway. I think." said James.

"I am still on the runway. Have to take off soon or else others will overtake." joked Avinash.

The next day Avinash was at the hotel the whole day. He did not call his parents even and did not go to shopping as well.

He came to downstairs in the hotel frequently to check the preparations for the party and found them to be satisfactory.

Decorations were made and dishes were prepared as per the orders of Avinash and he took personal interest in checking the menu prepared for the birthday party.

It was evening time and James came to the hotel where Avinash stayed and greeted him.

"Are you ready with your preparation?" enquired James.

"Mostly it is done. Hope there is no mess during the party." replied Avinash.

"Be cool. I know you can handle it smoothly." said James assuring Avinash to be confident.

Both James and Avinash were waiting while Avantika arrived.

She was wearing a pink color salwar kameez and was looking gorgeous. Avinash could not remove his eyes from her. She had kept her hair open which flew in the breeze and was looking extremely beautiful.

She greeted Avinash and James as she neared the table where both were sitting.

"It seems to be an expensive hotel." she said as she took her seat.

Both of them sat silently without saying anything.

"No it is not that much expensive as you think it to be." replied Avinash just to initiate the conversation.

"Well may I know why you invited me today?" asked Avantika.

"Don't you think it is a special day today?" asked again Avinash.

"Special day? Of what kind?" asked Avantika.

Without replying to her queries, Avinash directed the manager to bring the cake to the table and soon a waiter came there with a cake and placed it on the table.

"Happy Birthday Avantika." said both Avinash and James.

"I could not believe that you did it for me. I thought I am alone in USA so I could not celebrate my birthday this time but you made it really special for me." said Avantika so excitedly that tears of joy came through her eyes.

Avinash just at this moment placed the ring he brought a few weeks back on the table and said it was a gift for her on her birthday.

She opened the box and was surprised to see a small diamond ring.

"It might be so costly." she said.

Avinash simply smiled and said nothing. James smiled too but sat silently so that Avinash could take the lead.

"May I ask you something?" asked Avinash.

"Yes please." replied Avantika.

"Was opting for air hostess as a career your dream?" continued Avinash.

"Well, actually I wanted to be a pilot but the fees of training are so high that I could not afford it. So I opted for air hostess." she replied politely.

"My dream is to fly. It does not matter as a pilot or as an air hostess." she continued.

"But the question still arises regarding your job satisfaction." said Avinash.

"I am satisfied whole heartedly." she replied with a smile.

They ate the cake and after sometime Avinash offered to leave Avantika at her room and called a taxi.

James too went to his hotel and Avinash went with Avantika.

She did not speak anything during the drive and when they were about to reach the hotel, Avantika looked at Avinash and thanked him once again for the birthday party.

"Its nothing. I like doing such things." said Avinash.

"How did you know that it is my birthday today?" asked Avantika.

"Let that be a secret please." said Avinash smiling at her and she too smiled back and when the taxi reached the hotel, she opened the door, came out and bid goodbye once again to Avinash.

Avinash too bid her goodbye and asked the taxi to return to his hotel.

Avantika reached her room and took out the ring given as gift by Avinash and wore it in her finger. It fitted her perfectly as if solely made for her.

Avantika felt as if she is now attracted to Avinash after this birthday bash but ignored it assuming it to be an infatuation.

The next day Avinash boarded on duty along with James as usual.

"Did she tell anything?" asked James.

"Regarding what?" asked Avinash.

"I mean about post birthday party." said James.

"She just thanked me again when she got down the cab." replied Avinash.

Just as Avinash and James were talking to each other, the cockpit door opened and it was Avantika.

"Good morning sir." she greeted both of them.

"Good morning and have a nice day ahead." said Avinash.

Avantika showed him her finger showing the ring which he had gifted her the previous night.

"It fits me perfectly." she said with a smile.

"Oh so kind of you to say this." said Avinash gently.

The flight took off and after the journey landed at Mumbai.

Avinash came home, took a bath and tried to work on the flight simulation.

He sat on the chair but could not concentrate on the program. He could feel that his concentration is getting diverted but he could not tell exactly what the distraction is.

The harder he tried to concentrate, the harder it became. Each and every moment his mind would wander through the talks he had with Avantika. Her smile, the way she talked, her facial expressions etc.

Back at Mira Road, Avantika too felt the same. She could not concentrate on the work she was doing at home. Whenever she tried to do anything, image of Avinash would flash in her mind.

Avinash received a call from the British Airways office to collect his monthly duly schedule. He immediately went to the office and collected the sheet of papers which was his duty schedule for the month.

He saw that one of the trips this time was directed towards Singapore instead of USA.

May be the company itself is bored of sending me to USA again and again he thought.

"You have been given a duty as a substitute which means this will be the only trip you will be having to Singapore." said James

"I hope this one should be my last trip to Singapore." said Avinash.

"A pilot cannot have his own choice to fly and he is not supposed to select the trip according to his own will." continued James

"I know but still I would say that's my personal choice to go to US again and again. That's the country I love the most." said Avinash.

"Any change in Avantika's schedule?" asked Avinash doubting if she too had a different schedule or if she is coming to Singapore with him.

"Well, I will try to find out and will inform you. Mostly I don't think there will be a change in her schedule." said James.

As Avinash and James were talking, Avantika came. She seemed happier this time.

"You look so happy today. Anything special?" asked Avinash.

"This time I have got a schedule to go to London." replied Avantika.

Avinash and James looked at each other.

"But only once. Not more than that." she continued.

"When are you coming back to India?" asked Avinash

"After two days. What about you?" asked Avantika.

"I am going to Singapore this time and will be back after two day like the same way as you." replied Avinash.

As mentioned in the schedule Avinash left for Singapore and Avantika left for London.

They both did not contact each other either officially or unofficially as they knew they aer going to meet each other after two days.

Two days went by and Avinash landed at Mumbai on duty from Singapore.

Before he was to disembark from the plane, he received a call from the Air Traffic Controller.

"Avinash you are requested to come to the control tower immediately without any delay as there is an emergency." said the controller whose name was Rajat.

"Emergency? Of what kind?" asked Avinash.

"It has been reported that the pilots returning from London have fallen unconscious due to unknown reason and the plane is going to land in Mumbai in next two hours." he replied.

"What are you saying?" asked Avinash extremely shocked but still tried to be calm.

"Yes and I am serious. Can you do something?" asked Rajat.

"What do you want me to do?" Avinash shot back.

"Can you control the plane direct from the control tower?" asked Rajat.

Avinash thought for a moment and replied, "Before that we need to hold a meeting and make out a plan so that I could make out how successful we will be in this situation."

"Come to the ATC first and I will make arrangements for that." said Rajat.

Avinash rushed to the control tower. He saw that Rajat was there along with some other persons who were also involved in controlling of the planes from the control tower.

They all gathered in a room which was a part of the control tower and this was the place where meetings were conducted during emergency situations.

"I need list of crews in that plane." began Avinash.

"Wait, I will get it." saying so Rajat summoned another person and asked to get the list.

When Avinash was provided with the list, he went through the list and was shocked to see Avantika was too in the same plane.

"Avantika Sharma; is she the one who recently joined?" asked Avinash.

"Yes, she is onboard too." replied Rajat.

"Make arrangement for ambulances and fire engines as the plane would be making an emergency landing. The plane will go around twice before it makes an emergency landing. The passengers need not be informed of the emergency landing. Let them not know what is going on the ground. I want Avantika to take the control in the cockpit." Avinash said.

"She is new and has not any experience except serving." replied Rajat.

"Simply do as I say." shot back Avinash.

"Contact Avantika immediately and I will speak to her." continued Avinash.

Avinash took controls on the control tower and a contact with the plane heading from London was made.

"Hello, this is Avinash here. I need to speak to Avantika immediately." he began.

"Hello, Avinash. Avantika here. I am really afraid." she sounded as if she would cry sooner.

"Listen, don't panic. I am here to control the plane from Mumbai. You have still two hours to reach here." said Avinash trying to sympathize Avantika out of fear.

"But what about landing? Who's going to land it and how?" asked Avantika.

"It's you who is going to do it." replied Avinash.

"No way, I can't do it. Believe me, I am not a pilot like you." said Avantika whose voice choked.

"Listen to me first. Don't you trust me? If you are going to do as I say then definitely you are going to land smoothly without any accident." said Avinash.

"Just go to the cockpit and take the seat. I will instruct you what to do." continued Avinash.

Avinash began to instruct:

"Do you see two main displays? One is PFD and the other is ND and at the center is the DU?" asked Avinash.

"Avinash, this is too confusing. All I could see is only screens which display something or the other." said baffled Avantika.

"Cool down and don't panic. Don't let the passengers know about the situation. You will definitely make a smooth landing." assured Avinash.

"I got it what you say. Now continue but still I am not so much confident that I will land safely." said Avantika who was having her first experience in flying on her own.

"The information shownon the PFD is the airspeed tape, the altitude indicator, the altitude tape and the rate of climb indicator. Along the top, there is autopilot. Do you get what I am saying?" asked Avinash just to confirm if he is not rushing too fast even though that's the need of the hour

"Yes, I got it. The autopilot is ON now." she replied.

"Let it be like that only. Don't switch it off now but you need to do so just before the landing as you cannot land on autopilot." said Avinash.

Rajat saw Avinash as he wanted to make the landing in autopilot mode. Avinash gave a stern look at Rajat and indicated him to be silent and let him take the control as he wished. Rajat then sat silently.

"Avantika, listen what you see in the purple text near the autopilot is the autopilot speed." continued Avinash.

"Avinash, you know what you are saying is going as a bounce over my head. I am not getting a single sentence of what you are saying." said Avantika as she was more afraid of controlling the plane rather than crash landing.

"Simply listen. You are safe until you do as I say." continued Avinash.

"There is one little light above the PFD; this is a warning light that tells you when that the below-glidescope alert is active. Pressing the light inhibits the warning." said Avinash.

Rajat came to Avinash and said, "Are you sure she will be able to do it?"

"She will definitely do it if she concentrates just on my instructions. You just see how it is being done." he replied.

"Flying a plane is not a child's play, Avinash." shouted Rajat.

"Is letting the passengers die in front of your eyes a child's play?" asked Avinash.

Rajat went silent and did not know what to say.

"Do you see a well Avantika?" asked Avinash.

"I think I do." replied Avantika.

"Below the well there are three more lights. They light up to tell you when the speed brake is extended, and when the autopilot is failing to trim the aircraft properly."

Coming to the main point Avantika, The big round handle is the landing gear lever. Pull it up and the gear retracts; push it down and the gear extends. Above the lever are three landing gear lights. They are green when the gear is down, red when the gear is in motion or not fully extended, and unlit when the gear is up. It is typically a good idea to check for "three green" before landing." said Avinash who looked as if lecturing Avantika on flying.

Avantika now felt as if she is somewhat confident but yet she did not show enough courage on controlling the plane. But she had to do it as Avinash wanted her to do.

She followed Avinash's instructions and nearly after one and half hour, the plane was visible from the control tower.

"Avantika, do you see the airport in front of you?" asked Avinash.

"Yes, I do. When shall I proceed to land?" asked Avantika.

"Don't be in a hurry to land. Just go around twice. I will tell you when to land." Avinash instructed.

Avantika too was told how to control the plane through go around and now Avinash wanted the plane to land and he knew anything could happen if he commits a mistake here.

"Avantika keep your eyes on altitude indicator and let me know at what height are you at present." said Avinash.

"Avinash, it is showing 12,000 feet at present." she replied.

"Decrease the altitude but remember once you come below 10,000 feet altitude, switch off the autopilot." instructed Avinash.

Avantika closed her eyes for a moment as if praying to land safely and took on the controls.

She began to reduce the altitude and when she reached below 10,000 feet, she switched off the autopilot and informed about the same to Avinash.

"Now you are solely controlling the plane without any auto mode. Be careful. A single error can be a disaster." said Avinash.

"I will be more careful with your instructions." said Avantika.

As the plane came near the airport, its altitude gradually decreased.

"Avantika, now you are going to land. Be very careful. I have only time to instruct you on landing process and every instruction can be given only once. Be very attentive." said Avinash.

Avinash too was feeling nervous but he was helpless too.

"Check your landing gear and tell me the color of the lights displayed on the screen." said Avinash.

"I could see three green lights as you said." said Avantika.

"Perfect time for you landing then. As said before be careful. No sooner you will be landing." said Avinash and moved his hands indicating others in the control tower to get ready.

"Decrease the altitude slowly as you near the runway and keep informing me the altitude shown on the display." continued Avinash.

"10,000, 9,000, 8,000........." said Avantika as the plane came near the airport.

As she reached below 1,000 feet, Avinash asked Avantika to push the landing gear in order to release it.

Avantika followed the instructions and pushed the landing gear.

"You have crossed half of the well. You need to cross the other half." said Avinash.

Now the plane was nearly about to land.

"Avantika you are landing. Come on be calm and hold the jockey. Once the wheels hit the ground, retract the landing gear and the plane will slow down." continued Avinash.

Within minutes the plane landed and ran on the runway.

"Pull the landing gear now to reduce the speed. You have only 3 kilometers ahead of you to stop the plane." shouted Avinash.

"You can go up to 4 kilometers here." said Rajat.

"I want to stop as early as possible, so I instructed her to stop before she goes beyond 3 kilometers." said Avinash.

Avantika pulled the gear and the plane slowed down but was still running on the runway.

Fire engines and ambulance followed the plane from behind.

After running for somewhat more than 3 kilometers, the plane finally stopped.

There was a huge round of applause for Avinash in the control tower for successfully landing the plane.

Avantika was still in shock as she could not believe she did it.

The doors were opened and the airstairs were brought and the passengers embarked one after the other.

Avinash came down from the control tower and went towards the plane. He saw Avantika was coming down through the airstairs.

As soon as she saw Avinash, she ran to him and gave him a tight hug and began to cry.

"Thank you Avinash. Thanks a lot. Without you I could not be alive today." she began to speak with tears almost choking her.

For the first time, Avinash has been hugged by some girl and he glanced around to see if anybody was watching him.

The passengers nearby were looking at them. Avinash felt a little embarrassed.

"Avantika, we are still on the airport and people are watching us." he said to distract her.

"Let them watch. So what? You don't know what you have done to me. If I am here now at this moment, that's because of you." she said.

"But still it is public place." said Avinash.

Avantika looked at him for a moment and both went inside the airport to have some drinks.

They went to the restaurant and Avinash order two coffees for both of them.

"You know one thing landing a plane is like laying a child on the floor." said Avinash.

"You need to be as smooth as possible instead of hurrying." he continued.

"I am not a mother to lay a child on the floor and I don't have experience either." replied Avantika knowing that Avinash was joking.

"I am not a father either." said Avinash smiling.

"But you have experience of landing the plane." said Avantika.

21

"I land the plane as a pilot and not as a father. Whatever has happened to you today could happen even to me. Sometimes it may crash and in the more worse case, it will explode." said Avinash.

"That can happen to me as well." he continued.

The moment he said this, Avantika immediately kept her hands on his mouth in order to stop Avinash from speaking further.

"Don't talk like that. That cannot happen to you." she said as tears began to flow down her cheeks.

Avinash could not understand now why she is crying.

"Hey come on. That was a joke after all." he said patting on her shoulders.

"Even a joke can become serious sometimes. Please for me at least don't speak like that. I cannot listen to you speaking like that." Avantika seemed protesting.

"OK. Ok. I will not speak. But whatever I have said can be a reality. It is not necessary that the person sitting opposite to you speak always what you want to hear. Sometimes the reality is so harsh that you need to accept it and keep moving." said Avinash.

"Whatever you are saying imagine if it happened to me then what will be your response?" asked Avantika.

Avinash sat silently without saying anything because he could imagine such a thing should ever happen to Avantika.

After having the coffee, both left to their home.

Random thoughts ran through in Avinash's mind and various questions were rising in him.

"Was Avantika in love with him? Why did she not like him talking about being in an accident though it was imaginary? When he spoke about landing the plane like a child, she seemed to be shy rather than avoiding it?"

While thinking about all this, Avinash went to sleep unknowingly.

Avantika went to sleep too but could not sleep as the incident that occurred on that day kept running in her mind.

"What could have happened if Avinash had not returned from Singapore before her returning from London? Would there have been any other person to guide her in landing as the way Avinash did? Why did Avinash take the example of mother and child while explaining the landing of the plane instead of giving any other? Was he in love with her but still not making the first move?"

All these thoughts ran through her mind and she fell asleep.

Next duty for Avinash and Avantika was scheduled after four days. Both of them did not meet during these four days.

After four days, both left for USA on duty.

Just when Avinash entered his room at the hotel, he received a call from the reception.

"From whom?" he enquired.

"It's from Avantika." the receptionist replied.

"Hello." Avinash said attending the call.

"Hello, Avinash. I need a help of yours." said Avantika who was calling him from her hotel.

"Yes, what happened?" asked Avinash.

"Actually, the room where I regularly stay has been allotted to some VIPs and there are no vacant rooms here. I wanted to know if I can stay with you today." asked Avantika.

Avinash was on cloud nine. He was so happy that he could not give any reply to Avantika.

"Hello, you there?" asked Avantika.

Coming back to senses, Avinash replied, "Yes, you can. I will come there and pick you up."

Avinash hired a cab and went to the hotel where Avantika used to stay after duty.

As soon as he reached the hotel, he saw that Avantika was at the gate waiting for Avinash and as she saw him, she waved her hands.

Both Avinash and Avantika returned to the hotel where Avinash used to stay.

"She will be staying with me tonight. You prepare the bill accordingly." said Avinash to the girl at the reception smiling.

"Anyhow you are not gonna pay." she kidded.

"It's up to you." said Avinash winking his eye and look Avantika upstairs to his room.

"Your room seems to be more luxurious than mine." said Avantika who was excited to see Avinash's room at the hotel.

"It's official room and not a personal one and you too know that." said Avinash.

"But still you look the size of the room. It is big enough to accommodate more than four people or you say a family." said Avantika.

"Want to go for shopping?" asked Avinash.

"Really?" asked Avantika who was surprised to see Avinash asking her for shopping.

They both went to the New York harbor and in a boat went to Statue of Liberty.

"Oh my god! I cannot believe I am atop of Statue of Liberty. It's really unbelievable." exclaimed Avantika.

"But it is not a day dream. You have to believe it without any options available." said Avinash.

Both Avinash and Avantika took selfies and other photographs and spent nearly the whole day at Statue of Liberty.

At evening both of them returned and before going to the room, the both went into a hotel to have dinner.

"What would like to have?" asked Avinash.

"Whatever you will we having, I will have the same." replied Avantika.

Avinash order an Indian food and Avantika too had the same.

They decide to go by walk to the room as it was located nearby and they reached the room after a walk of nearly 20 minutes.

As they reached the room, Avinash took out his laptop and started typing.

Avantika went to have a bath and when she came out she saw him still typing on the laptop.

"Any important mails?" she asked.

"Not any. Why?" asked Avinash.

"I could see that you are so engrossed in your laptop from the moment we returned." she said.

"Actually I am writing about our visit to the Statue of Liberty." replied Avinash.

"You have habit of diary writing?" asked Avantika again.

"Yes, I note down about the visits I make, the kind of people I meet and others." said Avinash.

"The kind of people? Really?" asked Avantika as Avinash said he wrote about the kind of people he meets.

"I mean I write about the people who I meet daily." said Avinash shutting down his laptop.

"That means I can expect that you have written about me too." said Avantika who was curious and wanted to get more details from Avinash.

"Well some sort of." said Avinash after a pause.

"I would like to see what you have written about me please." exclaimed Avantika.

"Not now. I will show you when the time is right." replied Avinash ignoring her pleas.

Avantika went to sleep earlier while Avinash was still awake and it was nearly 1 am when Avantika woke up.

She saw that Avinash was sitting on the table and was talking to someone over the phone.

"Avinash, you are not sleeping?" asked Avantika.

He turned back and saw Avantika behind him.

"No, I am not feeling like sleeping. So I will not." said Avinash and continued to talk on his phone.

Next day, when Avantika woke up she could not find Avinash in the room.

She called the receptionist and asked her if Avinash had told her about him leaving the room and from the receptionist she came to know that Avinash had received a call from James to return to India immediately as his father was serious and had been admitted in the hospital.

Avantika now felt lonely as she had one more day to go to return to India on duty.

Avinash returned to Mumbai and called James.

"James, where are you now?" he asked.

"Avinash, you come to Taj Hotel immediately." said James.

"Taj Hotel? What are you saying?" asked Avinash who could not understand why James was called him to the hotel instead of hospital.

"Please come there and you will know everything." replied James and disconnected the phone.

Avinash immediately rushed to Taj Hotel and when he entered the reception and introduced himself he was asked to go to the second floor to the party hall.

"For whom the party is arranged?" asked Avinash to the receptionist.

The receptionist smiled at Avinash and told him to go to the second floor and find out himself.

Avinash went upstairs and was surprised to see his father standing with his friends and all were well dressed as if attending a function.

"What's going on here?" he asked baffling.

"Don't you remember it is your birthday today?" asked one of the guest.

"What's the date today?" asked Avinash.

"10th of August." replied his father.

"Oh! I forgot it. Believe me." said Avinash smiling.

He walked forward into the hall where he was hugged by the guests.

James was also present and he pulled Avinash aside.

"What happened?" asked Avinash.

"Does Avantika know that it is your birthday today?" asked James.

"May be she don't. I did not inform her. The first thing is I didn't remember myself." said Avinash.

"Inform her now." said James.

"But I don't have her contact number." said Avinash making a sad face.

Just as they both were talking, a voice followed from behind and Avinash turned back.

He was surprised to see Avantika standing in the banquet hall.

"Wish you many happy returns of the day." wished Avantika.

"I could not believe myself." said Avinash as this was the second surprise for him.

"How's the second surprise?" asked James who was behind all these surprises.

"When did you plan it?" asked Avinash.

"It was your father's plan and I executed it." replied James smiling.

There were songs played and more and more wishes poured on his birthday party. It was late night and the party was almost over.

"Avantika, I want to talk to you." said Avinash.

"Anything important?" asked Avantika.

"It is about your career." said Avinash.

"What is it? I am already an air hostess." said Avantika who was little baffled guessing what Avinash wanted to talk about her career.

"I don't want to beat around the bush. Let me directly talk the business. Why don't you undertake pilot training and make a career as a pilot?" asked Avinash.

"Not at all, I have already experienced once during that emergency landing. The horrific experience I will never forget." she said.

"It happened because you are not trained. Am I not flying by sitting in the same cockpit and make a safe landing every time?" asked Avinash.

"Let me remind you. Your initial interest was becoming a pilot and not an air hostess, if I am not wrong." continued Avinash.

"Let's assume that even if I opt for the training, then I don't have enough financial support to undertake the training." she said.

"James and I will support you financially. All you need to learn and interest in flying." said Avinash.

Avantika could not accept the request initially but could not reject it either. She finally nodded.

Next day, Avinash asked her to come to the Mumbai Flying School for registering her candidature.

Avinash had a friend who was named was Jagan and he was an instructor in the same school and he spoke to him in this regard and he readily agreed.

"If you don't mind, I want to instruct her whenever I am off duty." said Avinash to Jagan and he did not mind it.

Avantika came to the Mumbai Flying School at the appointed time and Avinash too was there.

He took her to the admission cell and spoke to Jagan and got her registered.

A medical checkup was carried on Avantika which was required for a person to qualify for a student flying license and her medical reports came positive.

"You can begin your training from next week." said Jagan.

Avinash took out his schedule and applied for rescheduling so that he could personally train Avantika.

His reschedule application was approved and Avinash informed about the same to Avantika and James.

A week passed and it was time for the training.

Jagan handed the parameters sheet to Avinash and took him to a Cessna which was a two seater plane.

Both Avinash and Avantika boarded the Cessna and Avinash took the controls.

The Cessna slowly moved on the runway and Avinash gradually increased the speed while on the runway and Cessna took off.

Avinash turned the plane towards the sea and as it was evening time, the view of sun set in the west was nice scenery to look from the sky.

"Avinash, why do you always turn towards the sea once you take off immediately?" asked Avantika.

"We do it on purpose and there is a reason behind that." replied Avinash.

"Why do we do it?" asked again Avantika.

"In case the plane develops any technical glitches immediately after takeoff, then it will be safe to crash on the sea rather than crashing on land." said Avinash.

"Do they happen most of the time?" asked Avantika who was more eager to know more.

"Well it does sometimes. It all depends on weather conditions." said Avinash.

"Leave it now and tell me one thing. What do you see in front of you?" asked Avinash.

"Well I could see the sun setting. That's all." replied Avantika.

"Anything else?" asked Avinash.

"The sea below is seen clearly separating the sky. I mean the zenith." said Avantika.

"Don't you think the zenith can described said in other words?" asked Avinash.

"How will you explain them?" asked Avantika.

"How about saying that both sea and sky are kissing each other?" asked Avinash.

Avantika turned towards Avinash and saw that he was smiling once he said that.

"Hmm. Not bad. A nice unexpected description." Avantika retorted.

"I have always seen it like that. This is what I call a flying kiss!." he continued.

Both Avantika and Avinash looked at each other but did not speak anything. It was a momentary silence.

"You are about to land. The runway is clear for you." came a voice from the air traffic control and Cessna landed and also the training for the day came to an end.

Avinash regularly trained Avantika in the coming months and now she was good enough to fly a plane alone on her own.

But she worked as an air hostess and always accompanied Avinash on duty.

Once while in USA, Avinash received an email from an unknown person whose name was Anvita and she claimed to have met him during her visits to USA often and had a purpose on writing an email to him.

Dear Avinash,

I am Anvita and I know that you don't know me. I have seen you many times while traveling to USA frequently and I am writing this letter asking for your support.

I am at present diagnosed with blood cancer and I am on an advanced stage. The day I saw you for the first time, I wanted to confess to you that you are most handsome person I have met but I postponed my confession as I wanted to know more about you.

I am sorry to say that I hired a private detective to get information about your whereabouts, what you do and if you are having any girl friends etc.

At present I am having all the information I want about you. In fact the email id of yours was also one of the information that was provided to me by the detective I hired.

I am not here to blackmail you for my personal gains as I am a business woman and money is not all what I need.

As I said before, I want to spend my last few days with you before I leave this world peacefully. Also I am attaching my medical reports.

Hope you will send me a positive reply.

Yours,

Anvita.

Avinash forwarded the same mail to James and asked his view on the mail he has received and what action should he take regarding the same.

James on seeing the mail responded to Avinash to support Anvita as her medical reports clearly indicates that she is on advanced stage and she may not cheat just for personal gains as mentioned in the letter.

Avinash responded to Anvita.

Dear Anvita,

I have not met you earlier but still I have decided to go ahead and support you by being present with you while not being on duty.

I will be coming to Mumbai tomorrow. We can meet at Morning Café at Dadar on day after tomorrow.

Hope to meet you soon.

Avinash.

Anvita's joy knew no bounds when she received a mail from Avinash and she was so happy that she forgot about her suffering from cancer.

Avinash left to Mumbai the next day on duty and reached home. All through the flight he kept of thinking about the meeting he is supposed to have with Anvita, a girl unknown to him until now.

The next day Avinash got ready to meet Anvita and left to Morning Café.

He entered the café and asked the receptionist if any of the guest in the name of Anvita has arrived.

The receptionist showed him a table in the corner and he saw a girl in her twenties sitting on the chair reading a book.

She was wearing a red mini skirt and her hair was loose. Her diamond studded earrings shone brightly in the lights.

Avinash went to the table and stood before Anvita.

She lifted her head up and saw Avinash standing before her and asked him to take a seat.

Avinash was shocked to see that it was no other than an air hostess whom he had seen many times during on duty to USA but had never spoke to her or even asked for her name.

"Are you not an air hostess?" asked Avinash.

"Yes, I am. I am too working in British Airways and have accompanied you many times to USA frequently." she replied.

"What about the letter you mailed to me?" asked Avinash.

"Yes, it is true that I am suffering from cancer but it is not true that I hired a private detective to get your information." she said.

Avinash ordered two coffees with biscuits of banana flavor and it arrived sooner.

Sipping the coffee, Avinash listened to what Anvita had to say.

"You know Avantika?" asked Anvita.

"Yes, why?" asked Avinash.

"When she joined as an air hostess, it was me who spoke about you to her. I was in love with you and I was to propose you but I don't know how or why you turned your interest towards her. I don't mind it nowadays as I am used to the way I am. In fact, I am happy that you have turned towards her as I am not in a position to live a longer life." said Anvita.

Anvita kept a diary on the table and said "Read this diary on the day when you get the news of my death. Please don't open it before."

The diary was black in color and looked somewhat old and Avinash put it in his bag without saying a word.

"Avinash, I want you to accompany me to the bars and hotels. Have dinner with me and spend your off duty time with me as much as possible. Though I have a little time to spend, I want to spend it as happy days of my life." Anvita said.

"Will you do it for me?" asked Anvita.

"I know it is a little harder for you to do as Avantika is with you nowadays and if you start ignoring her, she may leave you even." continued Anvita.

"It is not an issue for me. I will deal with her. I am ready to accompany you from now onwards." replied Avinash as he felt sympathy for her.

"Please don't disclose about my disease to anyone." Anvita pleaded.

"Avinash, you know one thing, this is the happiest moment I could feel." saying so Anvita took out her mobile and shot a selfie with Avinash and posted it on her facebook immediately.

Avinash knew that this post could be a backlash to him but he did not say anything as he wanted simply to keep Anvita as happy as possible.

After having coffee and snacks, both left the café. They decided to watch a movie. Avinash was not at all interested in watching movies as he had not seen many but still he accompanied to the talkies and both went to watch a romantic movie which was release recently.

While watching movie, Anvita said to Avinash, "Imagine what you would do if you and me were replaced in this movie as hero and heroine respectively?"

"I will be more romantic than the hero of the movie." said Avinash trying to bring a smiling face on Anvita.

"Really?" said Anvita and held his hands more tightly.

When the movie was over, both went to their home and Avinash was to report on duty that night.

Avinash reported on duty and Avantika was too there.

"Avinash, I have got my commercial pilot license." said Avantika and showed it to him.

"So you are free to fly commercial airlines as I do now." said Avinash smiling.

"Yes, I am. I owe you a party for that." saying so she invited him for a party and asked him to come along with James.

Avinash accepted the invitation and informed James too about the same.

Anvita took off from her duties for months and nobody seemed to bother about her except Avinash and James.

Avinash frequently contacted Anvita and used to enquire about her health which seemed to make her comfortable. All this was unknown to Avantika.

On the day of party, Avinash texted to Anvita that he is going to a party which has been arranged by Avantika and he will meet her the next day.

Avinash and James attended the party and Avinash thought it was the right moment to speak about Anvita.

"Do you know why Anvita is on leave nowadays?" asked Avinash to Avantika as if he had no knowledge about her.

"I don't know anything about her. Why are you asking?" asked Avantika.

"Nothing. I thought she might have told you about her absence." replied Avinash.

The next day again Avinash met Anvita at Morning Café as she had texted him the previous night.

"Hi, Anvita. I could see you are recovering well." said Avinash.

"It may seem so but it is not. Day by day it is getting worse. That's what the medical report says." said Anvita.

"I am planning to resign from my job soon as I know I will not be able to continue anymore." she continued.

Not knowing what to say, Avinash sat silently.

"What happened? Why are you so silent?" asked Anvita.

"Are you sure about your decision?" asked Avinash again.

"Yes, of course. I am going to submit my resignation tomorrow or day after tomorrow but don't worry I want you to accompany me until my last breath. Please." she pleaded.

"You need not say that. I am there always for you." convinced Avinash but he was still saddened about her condition.

He could see that whenever she spoke for too long, she would start coughing and would close her mouth with handkerchief and some drops of blood would be seen on it.

Avinash always tried to make it possible to let Anvita speak as less as she could. Sometimes when she could not speak, she would move her hands indicating what she required and Avinash could understand it.

It was Christmas weekend and the people of Mumbai were too busy in celebrating the week and that could be witnessed in the city bars. People would drink and enjoy the DJs until late night and would dance to the songs played in the bars.

Avinash and Anvita too decided to go to the bar and wanted to have some fun.

Avinash went to Anvita's home and took her in his car to the bar which was located at Santacruz.

They both entered inside the bar and already the celebration has begun. Some people were seen drinking while most of them were dancing to the music.

"Come on, let's have some drink and then we will dance too." said Anvita.

"I don't have the habit of drinking." said Avinash.

"Ok then, I want to drink. I would not compel you but you should at least dance with me." insisted Anvita.

"Of course, I will." replied Avinash.

Anvita ordered a drink for her and drank it at once.

"Do you think it is good for you to drink according to your medical reports?" asked Avinash.

"Whatever the medical reports say, I don't care. It is not going to be too long before this will end. Let me just enjoy every moment of my life." said Anvita as she drank another glass.

"Come on let's go and dance. You will enjoy too." she said pulling Avinash by hand and led him to the crowd which was dancing to the DJ.

Avinash too danced with Anvita following her steps closely.

Just when everything was going fine, unfortunately Avantika came from nowhere and Avinash did not notice that.

Anvita and Avinash both were enjoying the dance moves and were in their own world.

Anvita came along with some of her friends and she too did not drink while some of her friends did.

One of her friend pointed her fingers towards Avinash and asked Avantika, "Is is not Avinash over there?"

Avantika saw and tried to figure out to whom she was pointing and the person she was pointing was none other than Avinash.

"What is he doing here?" asked her friend.

"And who is the girl he is dancing with?" she continued.

Avantika lost her temper by now and went straight to Avinash.

"Stop it. You cheat." she shouted at the top of her voice.

The whole bar was silent not knowing what happened all of a sudden.

"I could not believe it Avinash. You are here with Anvita. You never told me about this relationship with her." continued Avantika.

"Avantika, it is not what you think it to be." said Avinash calmly.

"For how long have this being going on? You never spoke a word about it. It is me who believed you and trusted you blindly. I should not have done that. That's the biggest blunder I have committed in my life." shouted Avantika again.

"When I invited you to the party, you spoke of Anvita's absence. I grew suspicious about you the same moment but I did not ask you because I still believed you. But now you turned out to be a biggest fraud." she continued.

"Now onwards, don't try to contact me or meet me or try to be in touch with me. Forget me forever. Good bye." said Avantika and left the bar.

Avinash felt humiliated in the public and he whispered into Anvita's ear to leave the bar at once and she too agreed.

Once when they were in the car, Anvita spoke, "Avantika should not have spoke to you like that keeping in mind that it is a public place."

"She is not of that kind. She did so because she doesn't know about your medical condition and why I am with you." said Avinash.

"Even though she should have talked to you personally rather than shouting and insulting you in public." said Anvita.

"I will explain to her why I am with you without disclosing your condition and will see what happens next." said Avinash.

Next day it was a duty day for Avinash and he was sure that Avantika would be on duty too.

As expected Avantika was on duty and the moment he saw her, Avinash called out to her.

"Avantika, I want to speak to you." he said.

But Avantika left the place without paying any heed to him and this cleared signaled that she is ignoring him.

Avinash left the place without saying a word when he received a call from James.

"Hello", answered Avinash.

"I am sorry to inform you that Anvita is no more." he said.

"She was fine yesterday. What happened to her?" asked Avinash shocked.

"She had witnessed the fight between Avantika and you yesterday at the bar. When you dropped her at her home, she went inside and drank so heavily and then began to vomit blood. She was rushed to the hospital but she did not survive." said James.

"Shall I postpone my duty?" asked Avinash.

"You cannot postpone it at the last moment. You go to USA as usual. I will be here and will take care." said James.

Avinash boarded the flight but his mind was thinking about Anvita again and again that he that felt he is not able to concentrate on the controls.

In his bag, he always carried the diary that Anvita gave him during his first meeting with her and he decided to read it once he reached USA.

After landing at USA, he headed to the hotel and out of curiousness; he opened the diary given to him by Anvita and flapped the pages. He stopped suddenly in the middle and began to read:

I don't know what people think of Avinash but for me he is a dream boy. I don't know why I developed feelings for him all of a sudden but I confess it came naturally to me after once Avinash met me during one of the check-ins.

I was at the check-in counter giving the boarding pass to the passengers when Avinash came. A little girl of six or seven years may be gave him a rose as a thanking note though I think the girl had no idea who he was or whether they were to fly on the same plane.

"What will I do with it?" asked Avinash.

"Well, it is for you. I wanted to give it to a pilot and I felt like giving it to you, so I did." said the girl smiling.

"Thank you a lot." said Avinash who took the rose from her and headed towards me.

"This is for you." he said handing me the rose.

He very well knew I was watching all the drama that took place a few minutes ago but still this deed of him made me feel closer to him and I accepted the rose which he gave me.

After that he never met me personally.

Avinash is always social in nature not because his profession demands it but because he wants to be in touch with many around him including the passengers which his profession doesn't allow.

Even I was doubtful when I called him for the first meeting but he did came without questioning anything.

After revealing my medical condition, he promised me not to reveal it to anyone and also kept his promise even when his girlfriend humiliated him at the bar convicting him of cheating on her.

I know I will not live longer but I am sure if people have a person like Avinash with them, they need not look for any kind of support externally.

Avinash began to weep as tears flowed from his eyes after reading the above and closed the diary as he could not read ahead.

He slept that night at the hotel as he had to return to India the next day.

As scheduled he returned to India and discussed about the diary to James.

"This suggests that perhaps she was in love with you but did not speak to you about it as she already knew that she is suffering from blood cancer." said James.

"I will show this diary to Avantika. Let her also know the truth." said Avinash.

"Not now. She is scheduled to reach USA after four hours you reach New York next week. You may try to speak to her there. She will not behave like the way she did at the bar." said James.

"How do you know that?" asked Avinash.

"She is accompanying me this time to USA and the schedule difference is of four hours between yours and mine." replied James.

Avantika too was thinking of Avinash and the more she tried to forget him, the more his memories haunted her.

Avinash tried to call Avantika but she did not respond in spite of calling her many times.

Avinash texted her to meet him at New York once she comes to USA as he had to tell her the truth.

Avinash took off for New York and it was a smooth flight for him until he was about to land when he received a warning.

"The winds are blowing heavily. You may be required to postpone your landing." said the controller from Air Traffic Control (ATC).

"I will try to postpone but cannot do for a long time as the fuel is not enough to go more arounds." he replied.

"But you may try not to land sooner. The condition is worst here." came the response from the ATC.

"Shall I divert the plane to Dallas?" asked Avinash.

"It's far from New York. You land at New York. I will make arrangements." said the controller.

The plane went around the New York airport. Ambulances and fire engines were at the runway in case any emergency arises.

"You may land now. But remember the landing may not be safe." said the controller.

"I have no option but to land else I will run out of fuel anyway." said Avinash knowing that it is not worth to land now.

"I have no option other than to crash." Avinash continued.

"You cannot do that as that may leave the passenger meet unexpected things." said the controller.

After going two rounds over the airport, Avinash attempted the landing. The plane touched the runway but all of a sudden Avinash lost the control and the plane skidded off the runway. The engine caught fire and the smoke flew into the air.

"Avinash, reduce the speed. You cannot go ahead." shouted the controller from ATC.

But before Avinash could respond to ATC, the plane went totally out of control and hit the wall which was the boundary of the airport and exploded.

All of this happened in a moment before anything could be done.

Meanwhile, James was heading for New York and was supposed to land within few hours.

"You are diverted to Dallas, as a plane coming from India has crash landed at New York. You will soon be issued instructions for the same." said the controller to James and directed him to go to Dallas.

James became suspicious but did not express it to anyone and waited to land at Dallas and then planned to go New York to find out if it was not for Avinash.

Avantika was sitting on her seat when she saw someone standing at the galley of the plane.

"Who is there?" asked Avantika but there was no response.

She headed to the galley and saw that Avinash was standing there.

"What are you doing here?" she asked as she was surprised to see him here.

"Avantika, I wanted to speak to you but I think that it is not possible now." he said.

"What do you mean?" she asked.

"Forget it. Now answer me directly. Do you love me?" he asked.

Avantika did not say anything and stood silently.

"Avantika, I am asking again. Do you love me?" asked Avinash.

"Yes. I do. I love you." replied Avantika looking directly in his eyes.

Avinash came to close to her that there was only a gap of thin air between them.

Avantika felt like kissing him and she moved forward to kiss him. Suddenly she hit upon something and woke up.

"Oh it is only a dream. But it felt so real." she said to herself.

"Avantika, we are going to Dallas. You may announce it to the passengers as our plane is diverted to Dallas." said James to Avantika.

"Why? Are we not headed for New York as per the schedule?" she asked.

"Not because one of the planes has crash landed at New York." said James.

Avantika announced about the diversion to the passengers and the plane landed at Dallas after delay of two hours.

"You know where Avinash is now?" asked Avantika to James.

"Yes, why?" asked James.

"Because he asked me to meet him once I came to USA. He wanted to say something to me." she said.

"He is at New York now." replied James.

"Did a not plane not crash at New York a little before?" asked Avantika.

"Yes, I know but I too suspect that it may not be Avinash." said James.

"What are you saying? You mean to say that it's Avinash flight which crashed at New York." said Avantika who was in a shock now.

"I too don't know but I am going to New York immediate to check it out." said James.

"I too want to come with you." said Avantika and both of them boarded a plane to New York.

The flight took three and half hours to reach New York from Dallas. Once they landed, James went straight to the airport authorities to check out the details about the plane that crash landed that day.

People were seen crying and more medical personnel arrived at the airport and some were seen hugging each other consoling while most of them were at the enquiry counter to find out about their kin.

James asked for the name of the captain who was flying the plane and was said it was Avinash from Mumbai.

James could not believe what he got as a reply and he again confirmed the same.

"Sir, it is Avinash and the crash was so worse that it cannot be said whether if we could get any of his belongings or if Avinash is alive or not." said the person at the enquiry counter.

James officially applied to visit the crash site and his application was approved and he headed to the crash site along with Anvita.

There were broken parts of the plane on the runway and it was visible that the plane was burnt due to the fire and nothing could be found.

Medical personnel were taking the dead bodies of passengers from the debris. James saw the scene and he could not stand there for long as he did not wish to see Avinash in that state in which the passengers were pulled out from the debris.

Avantika stood silently dumbfounded. Her throat was choking and site was not worth seeing.

"Any clue about Avinash?" she asked to James.

"I don't think so." replied James who himself was saddened as he could not get any information about Avinash.

James found some bags which were burnt but the belongings were visible.

"Don't you think it belongs to Avinash?" asked James to Avantika pointing to a bag which was in the midst of other bags.

"Yes, it belongs to him. Let us collect it." said Avantika and went near the bag.

The bag was badly burnt and on the top two diaries was visible.

James lifted one of the diaries and opened it and saw that it was the diary written by Anvita. Avantika took the other diary from the bag and saw that it was written by Avinash. She began to read after flapping a few pages.

For the first time Avantika came to the cockpit and asked me if I would like to have something to eat. The way she asked politely was such that any person would have loved her for that.

I simply asked for coffee and perhaps that coffee itself was a turning point and Avantika and I became close friends.

Avantika continued reading.

I had nothing to do with Anvita but it was she who mailed me about her medical conditions and I promised to support her without disclosing her illness to anyone. In order to keep my promise, I had to hide it from Avantika but she mistook me and when she saw me at the bar with Anvita, she became furious and shouted at me and convicted me of cheating on her.

It was none of interest to cheat on her but I had to choose between Avantika and Anvita and I chose the latter as she needed my support more than the former.

I thought that Avantika was mature enough that she could go on independently but when she mistook me, she began to ignore me. I did not take it as humiliation because I know and I believe that she will not desert me after I reveal the truth behind me supporting Anvita.

I am going to tell her everything once she reaches New York after I land. Hope after hearing the truth, she will happily accept me. After all truth always triumphs.

Drops of tears from Avantika began to fell on the diary as she began to cry and felt guilty for ignoring Avinash.

"James, I want to meet Avinash immediately. Can you make arrangements for that?" she asked crying.

"It's too late Avantika. As per the list of names provided to me, Avinash could not be traced. May be he is burned to ashes as the plane has exploded." he replied.

"No, you are lying. You don't want me to meet Avinash." she yelled.

"Avantika, this is not the right time to joke. I am serious." said James who was wrecked on losing Avinash.

They went to the front end of the plane and saw that there were only ashes left and nothing could be found.

"Avinash why did you not tell the truth before?" shouted Avantika as she sat on the floor and lifted the ashes in her palms and began to cry loudly.

"Avantika, please stop. People are watching you." said James who too was weeping.

"Avinash, you could not do this to me. If you have told me or let me know what prevailed between Anvita and you, I would not have been like that." she continued.

But nothing was of use. Everything was over now.

James took the burnt diary and left the place.

Two years passed by and Avinash was almost a forgotten issue.

"Hello, This is Captain Avantika with my colleague Mr. James Matthews." announced Avantika who resigned her job as air hostess and joined as a pilot in the same airlines.

"Avantika, this shows you are grateful to Avinash even though he is not in between us now." said James.

"Whatever you say, Avinash has left a void in me which cannot be filled by anyone." she said.

Meanwhile at Edward Hospital, New York.

"Sir, Sir, come fast, the patient who was admitted two years back is now regaining consciousness." said the nurse to the doctor and the team of doctors immediately rushed to the room.

The patient was admitted two years back after a plane crashed at New York. When he was brought to the hospital, it came to light that he had already reached coma and it became difficult to reach to his relatives and the doctors waited for him to regain his consciousness so that they could find out about his relatives and inform them.

The only thing that they could recover from his shirt pocket was his passport which mentioned his name as Avinash.

"Hello, Mr. Avinash." said the doctor introducing him as Dr. Stephen Edwards.

"How do you feel now?" he enquired.

"I am fine. But how do know who I am?" asked Avinash who was not yet fully aware where he was and how he came here.

"We have your passport with us. Do you remember anything?" asked the doctor.

After being silent for a few minutes and trying to remember he spoke out, "Avantika."

"Avantika? Who is it?" asked the doctor.

"I don't know but that is what I could all remember." replied Avinash.

"OK OK don't put stress trying to remember your past. You may rest now. We will meet you later." said the doctor and left.

"Try to find out who Avantika is. Once we get to her, we will know more about him." said the doctor to the nurse.

Again when Avinash regained consciousness, he told that all he could remember is Anvita and Mumbai. Other than that he remembered nothing.

He asked the doctor to make arrangements for him to reach Mumbai.

"But where will you go in Mumbai?" asked the doctor.

"That I too don't know but once I reach Mumbai, I will at least find out my home." said Avinash and arrangements were made for him to go to Mumbai.

After spending one more week at the hospital Avinash left for Mumbai.

The Chhatrapati Shivaji International Airport was totally different this time that what Avinash saw two years before.

He had nothing with him as his bag was already burnt in the fire two years back and he was empty handed now.

As he walked down the airport, a voice from behind called him.

"Avinash?" said the voice.

He turned back and saw it was Avantika.

She came to him and hugged him tightly and began to cry.

"Where you have been all these years? I thought you were dead but thank god you came back. I knew you would not leave me alone but the plane that crashed made us believe that you are no more." said Avantika weeping.

"Promise me you won't leave me alone anymore." she continued.

James was too present but he did not want to interfere between them so he stood silently.

"I promise, I will never part you." said Avinash and they kissed each other.

*****THE END*****